SNOW INSIDE THE HOUSE

BY SEAN DIVINY

ILLUSTRATED BY JOE ROCCO

JOANNA COTLER BOOKS
An Imprint of HarperCollins Publishers

Snow Inside the House

Library of Congress Cataloging-in-Publication Data
Diviny, Sean.
  Snow inside the house / by Sean Diviny ; illustrated by Joe Rocco.
    p.   cm.
  "Joanna Cotler Books"
  Summary: A young child imagines what it would be like if it
snowed inside instead of outside the house.
  ISBN 0-06-027354-2.
  [1. Snow—Fiction.   2. Stories in rhyme.]   I. Rocco, Joe, ill.
II. Title.
PZ8.3.D6245Sn   1998   96-30723
[E]—dc20   CIP
                                                                  AC

Visit the HarperCollins Children's Books web site
http://www.harperchildrens.com
1   2   3   4   5   6   7   8   9   10
❖
First Edition

For Ramon "Babalooey" Balboa —SD

For Mandy "Foo Foo" Foster —JR

Snow, snow. Right out there!
Snowy ground and frosty air.
If it snowed inside here too,
think of all that I could do.

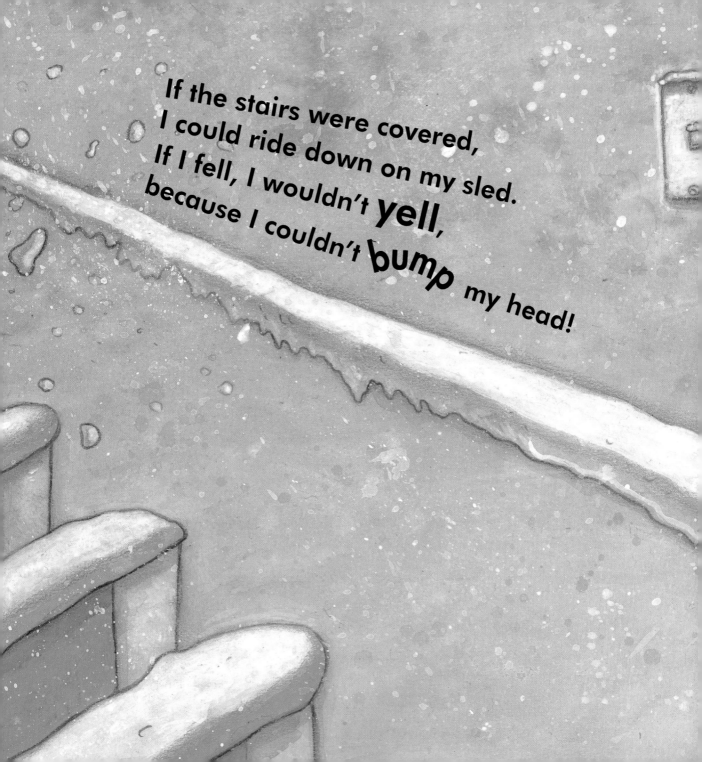

If the stairs were covered,
I could ride down on my sled.
If I fell, I wouldn't **yell**,
because I couldn't **bump** my head!

and to skate a figure eight

though the bathtub's mighty small.

SnOwmen in the living rOOm,
one in every chair. . . .

SnOwball fights on Monday nights
while Daddy's sitting there.

I would ride so **carefully**
upon my sn**O**wmobile . . .

Popsicles **galore!**
CHILDREN'S ROOM

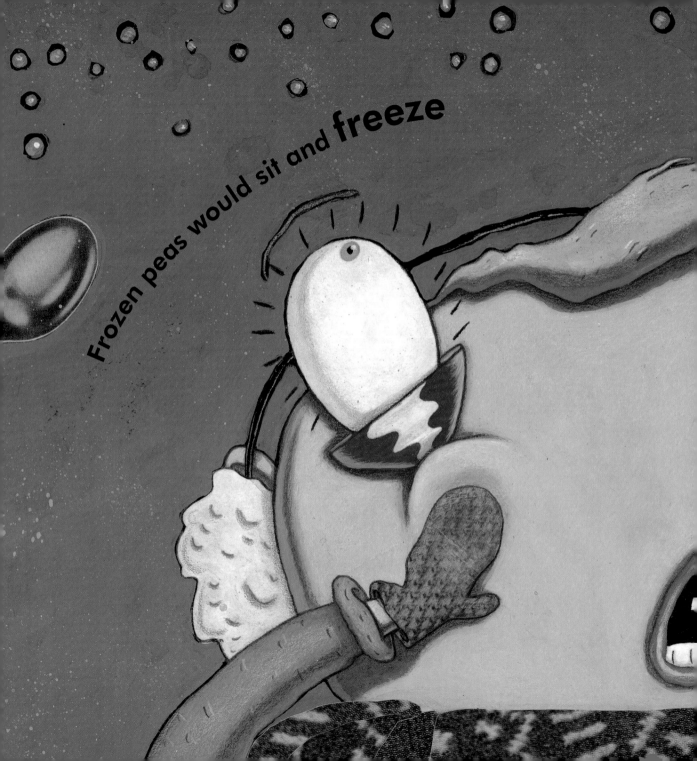

Frozen peas would sit and **freeze**

till **spring** arrived once more!

Chandeliers of icicles would **brighten** every face.

Gee, it would be sad
when we'd have to say gOOd-bye
But it might be fun to see
the ice-cube tears we'd cry.

Gee, it's **warm** and **cozy** under blankets in my bed.

Maybe I would rather have it snOw out there instead?

the w**O**rld all sn**O**wy white!